It's me, Parsnip

A lift-the-flap book by Sue Porter

MATHEW PRICE LIMITED

Someone
has walked through
a muddy puddle.

Someone
has made the cat door
all muddy.

Someone
has made muddy
footprints in the
kitchen.

Someone
has made muddy
footprints in the
living room.

Someone
has made muddy
footprints up the
stairs.

Someone
has made muddy
footprints in
Rabbit's room.

Someone
has made muddy
footprints in
the bathroom . . .

And now I'm lovely and clean.

THE END